Little Genie
A Puff of Pink

Little Genie
A Puff of Pink

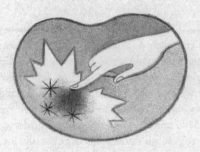

MIRANDA JONES

illustrated by David Calver

SCHOLASTIC INC.

New York Toronto London Auckland Sydney
Mexico City New Delhi Hong Kong Buenos Aires

ISBN-13: 978-0-439-89632-0
ISBN-10: 0-439-89632-0

12 11 10 9 8 7 6 5 4 3 2 1   7 8 9 10 11 12/0

Printed in the U.S.A.   40

First Scholastic printing, January 2007

Special thanks to Narinder Dhami

Don't miss these great books!

Little Genie

Make a Wish!

Double Trouble

A Puff of Pink

And coming soon:

Castle Magic

Contents

Chapter One
Six Reasons Why Mary O'Connor Is My Best Friend

1. She gave me her best BoyFrenzy poster—the one with the boys hanging out on a tropical beach—when the Bulldozer tore mine to shreds with his stupid plastic plane. (SORRY, I mean Jake, my sweet, charming little brother—*not*. Mom says I have to stop calling him the Bulldozer, but that's really hard because how else would you describe a six-year-old destruction machine?)

2. Her dad is way cooler than mine. Mary

complains when he tries to sing along to the radio, but at least he's *heard* of BoyFrenzy.

3. She doesn't have an annoying little brother, so her house is full of peace and quiet compared to this zoo. Okay, so her brother, Daniel, can be noisy too, and let's face it, all thirteen-year-olds are really weird, but at least he doesn't SHRED HER POSTERS with stupid plastic planes.

4. She lets me play with Nugget. Nugget always acts like there's nothing better in the whole world when you throw a stick for him. He doesn't always bring it back, but Mary says he missed that part of puppy school (hmmm, sounds like someone else I know! Are you reading this, Genie?).

5. She likes riding Splash Mountain as much as I do (well, almost).

6. She is absolutely nothing at all like Tiffany Andrews, Queen of Mean at Montgomery Elementary School.

Chapter Two
Blue and White and
Pink All Over

"Thanks for picking me up from school, Dad," Ali Miller called as she dashed through the front door and headed for the stairs.

"I've never seen you quite so eager to start your homework before," Ali's dad teased. "Are you sure you're feeling okay?"

Ali grinned. If her dad knew the real

reason why she couldn't wait to get upstairs, he'd be even *more* amazed. It had nothing to do with homework. It was because, after a long day at school, Ali couldn't wait to see Little Genie again! When Ali's gran had bought her an old Lava lamp at a flea market, Ali had never dreamed that she'd find a real, live genie inside.

"Genie, it's me," Ali called softly as she opened her bedroom door.

"Hey, Ali!" Little Genie was standing on the desk, waving. At the moment, she was the right size to fit into her Lava lamp home, about as tall as a pencil. "Watch!"

Ali gasped as Little Genie launched herself off the desk, her blond ponytail swinging. Her tiny hands gripped a paper clip hooked over a long line of thread. One end of the thread was tied to the Lava lamp on the desk, and the other was knotted around the leg of Ali's night-stand.

"Wheeeee!" Little Genie yelled. She whizzed down the thread, kicking her legs.

"Look out!" Ali warned as Genie got closer to the ground.

"Oh!" Genie landed in a heap on the carpet. She scrambled to her feet, shaking back her ponytail and smoothing her floaty pants. "That was fun."

"It looks like it," Ali agreed. "I wish I could try." Then she clapped her hand over her mouth. "Oops, does that count as a wish?"

Genie waved her wrist in the air. Her tiny, hourglass-shaped gold watch glinted in the sunshine. "It's all right. Your next set of wishes hasn't started yet," she told Ali.

Ali stared at Genie's watch. The top half of the hourglass contained a small pile of sparkling pink sand. The next set of three wishes wouldn't start until the sand began running to the bottom half. Ali could hardly wait.

She bent down to untie the thread from her nightstand. "What gave you the idea for this?" she asked.

"I saw it on that reality TV show we were watching last night," Genie explained.

"Oh yes," Ali recalled. The rest of her family didn't know anything about Little Genie, and it was really difficult for Ali to keep her a secret. Luckily, last night Ali's dad had taken her little brother, Jake, to a swimming party, and Mrs. Miller had been working on the computer in the dining room, so Ali had been able to sneak Genie downstairs in her pocket to watch TV.

"Would you like me to come to school with you tomorrow?" Little Genie suggested, beaming hopefully at Ali. "I could show you how to set up a zip wire in the hallway!"

"I'm not sure about that," Ali replied quickly, removing the thread from the Lava lamp. She remembered what had happened a week ago, when she'd had her last three wishes. Genie had made herself look like Ali and gone to school so that Ali could stay at home. But she'd got herself and Ali into a whole bunch of trouble. The school had nearly been washed away by a tidal wave, and Ali's classmates had nearly choked on Genie's hot-pepper cookies!

Although Ali loved having Little Genie

around, she had to admit that her friend wasn't very good at magic. Genie had already confessed that the teachers at Genie School had got so fed up with her causing mayhem, they'd shut her up in the Lava lamp so that she could spend some time improving her magic skills. As far as Ali could see, it hadn't worked at all.

"Someone's coming," Little Genie whispered at the sound of footsteps on the stairs. With a snap of her tiny fingers, she vanished in a small puff of glittering pink smoke.

Ali rushed over to the desk and sat down, opening her schoolbag. A moment later her dad came in.

"I brought you a snack." He smiled,

putting a glass of orange juice and a plate with a cheese sandwich on the desk. "Jake said his cartoons were making him hungry, and I thought you might like something too."

"Thanks, Dad," Ali said, opening her math book. Genie had vanished just in time.

"Well, don't work too hard," he said. "You know what they say about all work and no play!"

"Don't worry. I'm going over to Mary's later," Ali told him.

Her dad kissed the top of her head and went downstairs. Ali gave a sigh of relief. Then she jumped as Little Genie appeared out of thin air, sitting on the edge of the desk and swinging her legs.

Ali gasped. "I wish you wouldn't do that!"

"Invisibility classes were the only thing I was good at in Genie School." Little Genie grinned. "And speaking of school, you haven't said when I can come with you again."

Ali groaned. "Are you sure you want to?"

"Oh yes!" Little Genie winked. "Wasn't it worth it to see that major pain Tiffany Andrews get soaking wet?"

Ali had to laugh. "Tiffany was being even worse today," she said. She closed her math book. It was too hard to study when Little Genie was around. "She had her bedroom redecorated, and she was going on and on about how her mom got the most expensive designer in town to do it."

"What's it like?" Little Genie asked, resting her chin in her hands and looking up at Ali.

"Pink," Ali replied. "She keeps talking about her new striped curtains and new carpet and wallpaper with big pink flowers on it and *everything*."

Little Genie rolled her eyes and mimicked Tiffany's snooty voice. "You've got to see my new pink bedroom—it's really cool."

Ali grinned. "I'd like a new bedroom," she added, glancing up. The pale blue ceiling was painted with fluffy white clouds. Her curtains were white. On her bed was a matching blue duvet. "Gran decorated this for me when I was five years old. I wish I could liven it up a bit."

"Mmmm, I see what you mean," Genie said thoughtfully. "You need something a bit more groovy."

Plop! A drop of water splashed onto Ali's head.

"What's that?" Ali jumped to her feet and looked up at the ceiling again. Another drop of water splashed onto her face. Then another. And another!

"Oh no! What's going on? Is it that tidal wave again?"

Little Genie looked sheepish. "Um— no, it's the clouds on your ceiling!" she confessed. She held up her wrist, shielding the hourglass with her other hand to keep the raindrops off. "The sand must have started running through the hour-glass just before you made your wish to liven up the room," Genie explained. "Your room really *has* livened up!"

Ali pushed her wet bangs out of her eyes. Genie was right. Raindrops were falling from every cloud in the bedroom, including the ones on her duvet. But those raindrops were shooting straight *up*! Glancing around, Ali spotted her new red umbrella and rushed to put it up. Little Genie grabbed an empty CD case and huddled underneath it.

"Genie!" Ali shrieked. "I wish this would *stop*! That's my second wish."

"Don't you remember?" Little Genie replied. "You can't *unwish* a wish. You'll have to make another wish to change

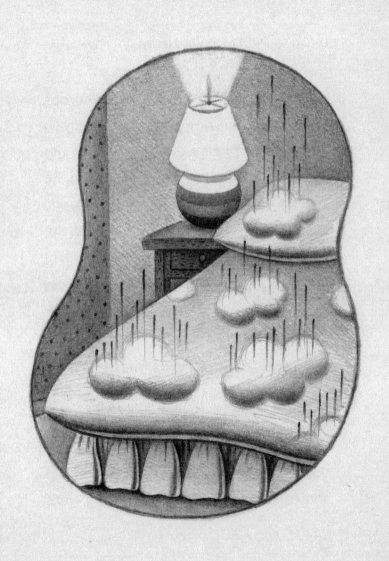

the room. That might make the rain stop."

Ali tried to think as cold raindrops dripped off the umbrella and ran down the back of her neck. Maybe *she* could have a new pink bedroom too. Knowing Tiffany, she'd probably gone completely over the top and had *everything* pink. Ali didn't want that. It would be like living in a cloud of cotton candy. And how on earth would she explain it to her mom?

"I wish—" Ali pictured a few things here and there—pillows, maybe, and a new lamp shade. "I wish I had just a *touch* of pink."

Immediately the rain stopped. Ali put down her umbrella with a sigh of relief and eagerly looked around. Where were the pink cushions and the lamp shade? There didn't seem to be a touch of pink anywhere. Everything looked the same, just a bit soggy from the rain. "What happened?" Ali asked Genie in a disappointed voice.

Genie looked puzzled. "I'm not sure," she said. "My fingers went all tingly like they normally do when you make a wish. And the sand in the hourglass didn't get wet. You must have got your wish *somehow*."

Ali shrugged. She ought to be used to Genie's magic going wrong, she realized. The most important thing now was to get everything dry again before her mom or Gran saw it.

Ali went over to the bed and felt the duvet cover. "It's not too wet," she began.

Then she frowned. "Hey! What's that?"

There was a bright pink mark on the duvet cover, in exactly the place where Ali had touched it. As Ali and Little Genie watched, the pink spot grew bigger.

And bigger. And *bigger*.

The pool of dazzling pink spread and spread to all four corners of the bed. In ten seconds, Ali's pale blue duvet cover with fluffy white clouds was bright pink all over.

Chapter Three
Sandwich Basketball

"My duvet!" Ali stared down at her bed in amazement. "It's pink!"

"It looks great." Little Genie beamed. "I love pink."

"But it was blue," Ali said in a daze. "And now it's *pink!*" She put her hands on her hips and swiveled to glare at Little Genie. "What's going on?"

"Well, you did ask for a *touch* of pink," Genie reminded her. She grinned and pointed at Ali's jeans. "And now your clothes look really cool too!"

"What?" Ali gasped. She took her hands off her hips and looked down at herself. Her blue jeans and white tank top had turned the same dazzling pink as her duvet.

Ali blinked. "D-does this mean that everything I touch will turn bright pink?" she stammered.

Little Genie nodded. "Isn't it great? But I wouldn't touch your hair if I were you."

Ali had just been about to push her bangs off her face once more. Now she kept her hands firmly by her sides. "This is the worst thing *ever*," she groaned. "What am I going to do?"

"Don't panic," Little Genie said helpfully. "The wish won't last forever."

"Yes, but we don't know how long I'm going to be like this!" Ali pointed out. The wishes lasted as long as it took the sand to run through Genie's hourglass watch. But since the hourglass worked on magical Genie time, neither Ali nor Genie knew when the wishes would end.

"Calm down," Genie soothed her. "Why don't you have that snack your dad brought you?"

Ali nodded and picked up the glass of orange juice. To her dismay, the juice turned bright pink as soon as her fingers touched the glass.

"Don't touch the plate," Genie warned. "I'll feed you." She used both hands to break a bit off a corner of the sandwich.

"I'm not really hungry," Ali began, but

Genie bent her knees, jumped up, and threw the bit of bread and cheese toward her. Ali opened her mouth to protest, then gulped as the bread landed neatly on her tongue.

"Hey! This is just like playing basketball!" Genie exclaimed, pulling off another piece. She was about to throw it when Ali heard something outside and turned around. A car had pulled into the Millers' driveway.

"Rats!" Little Genie said crossly as the bread whizzed past Ali's cheek. "You have to keep still, you know."

Ali rushed over to the window. She pushed the curtain aside and looked out. "It's my mom," she said. "She's home from work." Then she groaned as bright pink spread rapidly across the blue and white curtains. "I've done it again!"

"Well, you *did* want a pink bedroom just like Tiffany Andrews," Genie reminded her rather indignantly. "And now you've got one."

"Hi, everyone, I'm home," Mrs. Miller called from the hall. Then Ali heard her mom coming upstairs.

"Oh no," Ali breathed. "Genie, you'd better disappear."

"I'm just going," said Genie cheerfully. "But remember—don't touch your mom, or she'll turn pink too!"

Genie vanished, and Ali found herself glaring at thin air. She took a deep breath as she heard her mom reach the top of the stairs—and then she nearly jumped out of her skin! Genie had reappeared, dancing up and down on the desk and pointing at the glass of pink juice.

"You'd better hide this," she whispered.

Ali dashed across the room and pushed the glass behind a pile of CDs. She turned around just as her mom came in.

"Hello, honey," her mom said. "Did you have a good day at school?" Then she stepped backward in surprise. "Goodness me! Pink curtains! And a pink duvet cover! Where did *they* come from?" She looked at Ali. "Has Gran been shopping again?" she asked.

Ali called her gran the Junk Queen because she loved flea markets, garage sales, and thrift shops. Her tastes were a bit strange, though, and she often gave

Ali and her mom secondhand bargains that were pretty hideous.

Ali opened her mouth to say yes but then thought better of it. After all, if her mom decided to ask Gran about the curtains and duvet cover, things could get pretty tricky! "Um—Tiffany Andrews lent them to me," Ali explained, staring down at the carpet. "She's just had her bedroom done in pink, and she let me borrow these so I could see how the color looks in my room."

"Tiffany Andrews?" Mom raised her eyebrows. "That was kind of her. I thought you two didn't get along that well. You'll have to invite her to play sometime."

"Okay," Ali mumbled. *No way!* she thought.

Mrs. Miller was looking around the room, but luckily she hadn't noticed that the carpet and the duvet cover were suspiciously damp. "I suppose it *is* about time we redecorated in here," she remarked. "And if you want a pink bedroom like Tiffany's, that's fine. We'll paint it during the school holidays."

Ali tried to smile at her mom, but if there was one color she *didn't* want in her bedroom now, it was pink.

"And where did you get those clothes from, Ali?" her mom went on, suddenly noticing Ali's jeans and tank top. "I don't remember seeing those before."

"Oh, I found them in the back of my closet," Ali said, thinking quickly. "I haven't worn them for ages." She breathed a sigh of relief as her mom went over to the door.

"By the way, do you want a ride over to Mary's tonight?" asked Mrs. Miller.

"Um—no thanks, Mom," Ali replied. "I'll walk." She wasn't sure her mom would be too pleased if her cool silver car suddenly turned bright pink—which is what would happen as soon as Ali touched the door handle!

Mrs. Miller nodded and went downstairs.

"Genie!" Ali whispered. "Where are you?"

"Over here," Genie called, appearing cross-legged on Ali's pillow. "Well, that didn't go too badly, did it? I think I'd better come with you to Mary's, though. You might need my help."

Ali raised her eyebrows. "*Your* help?"

she echoed. "You're the one who got me into this mess!" Anxiously she glanced at the hourglass on Genie's wrist, but only a few grains of sand had trickled through so far. Ali sighed. It looked like her wish was going to last for a long time.

"But the pink looks lovely," Genie insisted, bouncing on the pillow. "It's my *favorite* color. Lots of nice things are pink—like bubble gum and cotton candy and roses and the sky at sunset. . . ."

"That doesn't help," Ali grumbled. "Just tell me how I'm supposed to go to Mary's house and not turn anything pink?"

Genie bounced so hard that she flew into the air and did a somersault like a gymnast. "Whoopee! I'm pretty good at this, don't you think? You could always phone and tell her you can't come," she suggested as she landed on the pillow.

"Good idea," Ali agreed eagerly. Then her face fell. "No, I can't do that. I'd have to touch the phone, and it would turn pink."

"Then you'll just have to go," Genie advised. "But don't touch anything. And wait for me! I won't be long." She vanished, leaving just a puff of pink smoke behind her.

"Don't touch anything?" Ali repeated, frowning. "How am I supposed to do that?" She reached out to pick up her green backpack. In a flash it turned bright pink. Ali shook her head and sighed. It was *impossible* not to touch things.

Whoosh! Little Genie appeared on Ali's pillow again. Instead of wearing her usual genie clothes, she had changed into jazzy pink pants and a sparkly jacket. Her ponytail holder glittered with pink jewels.

"What do you think?" She beamed,

striking a pose. "With all this pink around, I didn't want to feel left out."

"Very nice," Ali said. She couldn't help smiling as Genie strutted up and down the bed like a supermodel. "You'd better let me put you in the backpack."

She reached out, but Genie leapt back. "I know I love pink, but I don't want to *be* pink!" She grinned. "I'll get into the backpack myself."

Well, that's nice, Ali thought a bit crossly as she put the backpack on the bed and watched Genie wriggle into the pocket. After all, it was all Genie's fault that she had a touch of pink. And was she *really* going to be able to visit Mary without touching anything? Ali was beginning to feel very, very worried.

Chapter Four
Flower Power

Taking a deep breath, Ali slung her backpack over her shoulder and went out of the bedroom. "Don't touch anything," she whispered to herself. "Don't touch *anything*." Just to make sure, she jammed her hands tightly into the pockets of her jeans.

"Remember, don't touch anything," Genie said, popping her head out of the backpack pocket as Ali reached the top of the stairs.

"I know," Ali told her. "And don't make such a fuss—you're making me nervous!"

Genie winked at her. "Just trying to help," she chirped, disappearing into the pocket again.

Ali walked downstairs, feeling as if she was treading on eggshells. She remembered not to touch the walls or the banisters, but by the time she got to the bottom, she was feeling quite worn out with worry. How was she going to make it all the way to Mary's? Then she remembered something else and groaned loudly.

"What's the matter?" Little Genie peered out of the pocket again.

"How am I going to open the front door?"

"Ask your mom or dad to do it for you,"

suggested Genie. The kitchen door at the end of the hall was half open, and they could hear Ali's mom and dad chatting.

Ali shook her head. "They'll think I'm nuts," she whispered.

"Hold on! Fab idea alert!" Genie craned her neck and beamed up at Ali. "I'll make myself full size so I can open the door for you, and then I'll make myself small again. Simple."

"No, Genie, it's too risky—" Ali began. At that moment, the kitchen door opened and her dad came into the hall. Little Genie quickly ducked out of sight.

"I'm headed to the gym," he said. "Do you want a ride to Mary's?"

"No thanks, Dad, I'm fine," Ali replied. "It's such a lovely day, I'd rather walk."

Her dad looked a bit surprised. "Okay. See you later, then." To Ali's relief, he opened the front door just ahead of her. Ali scurried after him.

"Don't be too late, Ali," her mom called as she shut the door behind them.

"Okay, Mom," Ali said.

So far, so good, Ali said to herself as her dad held the garden gate open so that she could go through. She waved as he got into his car and drove off with a toot of the horn. *Maybe this won't be too difficult after all,* Ali thought.

"Hello, Ali. How are you?"

Ali turned to see their neighbor Mrs. Carter standing in her front yard. She had a trowel in her hand.

"I'm fine, thank you," Ali replied. She

went over to the fence, being careful not to touch it. "How's Marmalade?" Marmalade was Mrs. Carter's handsome but very timid ginger cat.

"He's fine." Mrs. Carter beamed. "And you know, he's so much braver now than he used to be. He doesn't get chased by the other cats at all."

Ali grinned. What Mrs. Carter didn't know was that it was all thanks to the little cartoon tiger Genie had brought to life for Ali's first wish. The tiger had frightened all the neighborhood cats away with his deafening roar!

Bzzzzz!

Ali jerked sideways as a bee flew right in front of her face. As she flapped her hand to scare it away, she brushed against the blue flowers that were over by the fence. To Ali's horror, all the flowers immediately turned bright pink!

Mrs. Carter didn't notice. She was too busy looking round the garden. "Now that I think of it, I haven't seen Marmalade for a little while," she said with a frown. "I wonder where he is."

"Well, I'd better be going," Ali said quickly. She was just about to turn away when Mrs. Carter let out a shriek.

"Oh!" she gasped. "Look at those pink flowers!"

"Um—yes, lovely, aren't they?" Ali stammered. She saw Little Genie pop her head curiously out of the pocket for a moment and then dive back inside, a grin on her face.

"But that plant is only supposed to have *blue* flowers. I've never seen a pink variety before. What a wonderful surprise!"

Ali managed a smile. She could feel her cheeks burning as pink as the flowers. Still, Mrs. Carter seemed to like them.

"Maybe I should call that gardening channel on TV and tell them I've got a brand-new species of flower growing in my garden," Mrs. Carter went on eagerly.

"Perhaps they'll even come and film it!"

"That might not be such a good idea," Ali began. After all, when the wishes were over, the pink flowers would turn blue again. But she didn't get a chance to say anything else, because just then a miserable yowl interrupted them.

Miaoooooow!

Instantly Mrs. Carter forgot about the flowers. "That's Marmalade!" she exclaimed. "Where is he?"

Ali looked up. Marmalade was crouched on a branch high in a tall tree.

"Marmalade!" Mrs. Carter rushed over to the tree and gazed up at her ginger cat. Ali and Genie followed her. "Are you stuck?"

Marmalade mewed loudly.

"Oh dear, I think he *is* stuck," Mrs. Carter said.

Little Genie poked her head out of the backpack pocket. "Poor Marmalade," she whispered to Ali.

"If I fetch my stepladder, will you climb up and get him, please, Ali?" asked Mrs. Carter. "I'm not very steady on my feet these days."

Ali was just about to agree when a thought struck her. The second she touched Marmalade, the cat would turn pink! "I can't, Mrs. Carter," she said, searching desperately for a good excuse. "I'm—I'm scared of heights."

"But we've got to do *something*," Genie whispered. She had become good friends with Marmalade since the incident with the purple tiger. "Ask Mrs. Carter to go inside and fetch some of Marmalade's favorite cat treats. Then maybe I can do some magic to help him while she's out of the way."

Ali bit her lip. Knowing Little Genie, anything could happen! On the other hand, she agreed that they had to do something to help. "Maybe we can tempt Marmalade down with some of his favorite treats, Mrs. Carter," she said out loud.

"That's an excellent idea. I'll get some right now." Mrs. Carter hurried into the house.

Ali put the backpack down on the grass, and Genie climbed out. She had taken off her jacket.

"What are you going to do?" Ali asked. But Genie had already closed her eyes and was whispering a spell. Ali could only catch a few words of it. ". . . *bouncing high, jumping up into the sky . . .*"

There was a puff of white smoke. Ali blinked. A small, round mini-trampoline had appeared under the tree.

"Please tell me you're not going to do what I think you're going to do." Ali groaned, shaking her head.

"Well, I don't know what you think I'm going to do," said Genie as she climbed onto the trampoline. "But I'm going to jump on the trampoline and bounce myself right into the tree." Marmalade was staring down at them, purring now that he'd spotted his friend. "Then I can help Marmalade down."

"That's exactly what I thought," Ali

muttered. This was yet another of Genie's wild ideas!

"You've seen how good I am at bouncing on your bed," Genie said, beginning to jump up and down. "And this is a magic trampoline, so I'll be able to go even higher. Wheeee!"

Ali held her breath as Genie shot up into the air. *Boing! Boing!* She bounced

closer and closer to the branch where Marmalade was sitting, but not quite close enough. The trampoline sent her soaring into the air a third time, and this time Genie managed to grab the branch and climb onto it.

Marmalade looked very pleased to see her. He purred even more loudly and rubbed his head against Genie.

"Careful, you'll knock me off the branch!" Genie laughed. She stroked Marmalade's ear.

"Are you okay?" Ali called, peering up into the tree.

"I'm fine." Genie shaded her eyes and looked at Ali. "Um—it's a long way down, isn't it?"

"You'd better hurry up," Ali warned her.

44

"Mrs. Carter will be back any minute."

Genie was still staring at the ground. "It's a long, *long* way down," she said in a wobbly voice. Then she gulped and put her hand over her eyes. "You know what, Ali? I just remembered. *I'm* scared of heights!"

"What?" Ali exclaimed. "You can't be!"

"I am," Genie moaned. She crouched down on the branch and wrapped her arms around Marmalade's neck. The cat licked her cheek.

"But you're a genie," Ali pointed out.

"I know, but genies can be scared of things just like anyone else," Genie said. She was trembling all over.

Ali groaned. They were in a real pickle!

"Stay still, Marmalade!" Genie cried out

in alarm. The ginger cat had wriggled free and was padding away from her along the branch. "Don't leave me."

Marmalade stopped, still purring, and stroked Genie's face with his fluffy tail. Then he set off again. He walked to the end of the branch and jumped neatly down to the one below.

"Genie, he's showing you the way down," Ali called, relief flooding through her. "He wasn't stuck after all. Can you follow him?"

"I'll try. But my knees are all wobbly," Genie complained, getting to her feet. She crept cautiously along the branch and climbed down to where Marmalade was waiting for her, his head cocked to one side. Then the ginger cat set off again.

Marmalade made his way down the tree branch by branch. He kept stopping and waiting for Genie to join him until they had climbed down to the lowest branches. Then Marmalade jumped lightly to the ground and sat down to wash his ruffled fur.

Ali held up the backpack so that Little Genie could climb straight back into the pocket. She'd just slid down out of sight, her ponytail messy and her pink pants covered with leaves, when Mrs. Carter hurried out of the house with a box of cat treats. A second later the trampoline vanished into thin air.

"Sorry I took so long," Mrs. Carter panted. "I couldn't remember where I'd put these." She stopped when she saw

Marmalade sitting on the lawn, licking his paw. "So he got down on his own after all, did he? What a clever boy! First he scared off all those cats, and then he climbed up that enormous tree!"

"Yes, he's something," Ali agreed. "I've got to be going now, Mrs. Carter. I'll see you later." She hurried out of the garden and along the street. When she was safely out of sight, she stopped and peeped into her backpack. "Genie, are you okay?" she asked in a low voice.

Genie was lying in the bottom of the pocket, fanning herself with her hand. She smiled weakly at Ali. "I'm fine," she said. "Phew! That was scary."

"Just don't get any more bright ideas like that," Ali said firmly.

Five minutes later Ali reached the O'Connors' house and breathed a sigh of relief. She'd made it—and she'd managed not to turn anything else pink along the way. Luckily the O'Connors' front gate was wide open, so she didn't have to touch it. Mr. O'Connor was always going on at Mary to shut the gate behind her so that Nugget didn't get out. But now Ali was very glad her friend hadn't taken any notice.

I'm doing pretty well, Ali thought proudly as she walked up to the front door. Then her face fell. "Oh no!" she said under her breath.

Chapter Five
Wash and Dry

Genie stuck her head out of the pocket. "What's the matter?" she asked.

"How am I going to ring the bell?" Ali pointed at the doorbell. "I'll turn the whole door pink."

"Just shout, *'Mary!'* really loudly," suggested Genie. "She'll hear you and open the door."

"Yes, and so will all the neighbors," Ali protested.

"All right, hold up the backpack and *I'll* ring the bell," said Genie.

Ali lifted the backpack up and Genie leaned out of the pocket toward the bell. She pressed it, but Ali didn't hear any chimes. "You'll have to do it harder," she whispered.

"Okay," Genie panted. She put both hands on the bell, took a deep breath, and pressed it again with all her strength. This time Ali heard a faint ring inside the house. Huffing and puffing, Genie slipped back into the pocket a split second before Mary opened the door.

"Hi," Ali said. "Sorry I'm late."

"That's okay," Mary said.

"What's up?" Ali asked as she stepped into the house, making sure she didn't touch the door or Mary on her way in. "You look a bit stressed."

Mary rolled her eyes. "Daniel is driving me crazy!"

Ali couldn't believe that Daniel could possibly be more annoying than the Bulldozer.

"What's he done now?"

Mary looked embarrassed. "We had this bet," she explained. "You know how he's always got lots of girls chasing after him—or so he says."

Ali nodded. Every time she saw Daniel, he seemed to have a different girlfriend.

"Well, he gave his phone number to a girl he met on the bus. I bet him she wouldn't call," Mary went on. "And she *did*. So that means I lost."

"What did you bet?" Ali asked.

"I have to wash his dirty soccer jerseys and shorts." Mary made a face. "And not just his—it's Daniel's turn to do his team's laundry. So I have to wash his teammates' stinky old jerseys too!"

"Yuck!" Ali wrinkled her nose. "Can't you get out of it?"

"No." Mary sighed and led the way to the kitchen. "My mom says a deal's a deal. All the stuff's in the dryer right now, and Daniel's running around yelling because he's got a match in an hour. Can you help me?"

Ali gulped. "Okay," she mumbled, hoping she wouldn't have to touch anything.

"By the way, I like your new backpack," Mary said, glancing at Ali. "And your new pink clothes. Don't tell me you've turned into Tiffany's biggest fan," she teased.

Ali shook her head. "Actually, I've decided I don't really like pink that much," she said glumly.

The radio was on. Mary's dad was making a cup of coffee. He grinned at Ali. "Hi, how're you doing?" he said. "What do you think about Mary doing Daniel's washing? Pretty impressive, huh?"

"Well, I'm not doing it again," Mary said. She went over to the small laundry room next to the kitchen. The clothes in the dryer were still spinning around.

"Hello, Mr. O'Connor." Ali carefully put her backpack down on the table.

"Hey, this is my favorite!" Mary's dad stopped stirring his coffee as a song

started to play on the radio. He began snapping his fingers and swinging his hips. "It's the new BoyFrenzy single. Have you heard it, Ali?"

Ali couldn't stop giggling. Mr. O'Connor was really funny! Mary didn't think so. She shook her head as her dad danced around the kitchen singing, *"Don't leave me, baby! Please say you'll never go away!*"

Suddenly Ali heard a noise behind her. It was coming from the backpack. Genie was humming the tune along with Mr. O'Connor. "Shhh, Genie!" Ali shushed under her breath. She looked up to find Mary staring at her.

"Don't join in!" Mary told Ali. "It just makes him show off even more."

"Um—sorry," Ali said. At least Mary thought *she* was the one who was humming. Ali glanced at the backpack, hoping that Genie would take the hint and be quiet. But then Ali saw that the backpack was beginning to twitch. Genie was obviously doing some of her favorite dance moves!

There was only one thing Ali could do. Feeling very embarrassed, she began to dance about in front of the table, hiding the backpack with her flailing arms and shimmying hips.

Mary covered her eyes.

"That's great, Ali!" Mr. O'Connor laughed.

The song ended at last. Her cheeks bright red, Ali glanced anxiously at the backpack. It had stopped moving. With a sigh of relief, she firmly zipped the pocket.

Mary shook her head at Ali as her dad picked up his coffee and went out. "Please don't dance with him," she said. "It only encourages him!"

Ali didn't get a chance to reply because at that moment Daniel stuck his head around the kitchen door, his cleats slung over his shoulder. "Is my stuff ready?" he asked.

"Not yet," Mary said with a scowl.

Daniel frowned. "Well, I haven't got time to wait for it," he said, glancing at his watch. "I'm in a hurry. You'll have to bring it to my practice."

"What?" Mary put her hands on her hips and glared at her brother.

"I told you, I'm in a hurry. Dad's coming to the match, so he can help you carry it."

"I suppose you want to get there early because *Julie's* going to be there," Mary teased. Ali smiled as Daniel turned bright red.

"Just don't be late," he snapped, and

stomped down the hall. A second later they heard the front door slam.

"What a pain!" Mary grumbled. "Now we're going to have to go to a stupid soccer match. If he could have just waited two minutes, everything would have been ready." She bent down to open the dryer. "Sorry about all this, Ali."

"No problem," Ali said. She couldn't think of anything she'd have to touch as she was standing on a playing field, and maybe the wishes would have worn off by the time she got home.

"Mary, could you come here a minute?" Mr. O'Connor called from the living room.

Mary made a face. "I never get a minute's peace around here!" She sighed.

"Will you get the washing out for me, Ali?"

"Sure," Ali replied without thinking.

As Mary went out of the kitchen, Ali glanced over at the backpack. It was twitching again. Genie was probably trying to get out. Well, after forcing her to dance around like that in front of Mary and her dad, Genie could stay zipped up in the pocket for a bit, Ali decided with a grin. She knelt down in front of the dryer and put her hand inside.

Little Genie's voice came faintly from inside the backpack. "Ali! Don't touch anything!"

But it was too late. Ali gasped in horror as she watched the bright pink color spread from her fingers through the jumble of blue and white shirts and shorts inside the machine.

Now the shorts were a shocking pink, and the shirts were pink with purple stripes!

Chapter Six
Something Red

Ali stared openmouthed at the jerseys.

"You touched the clothes, didn't you?"
Little Genie called from inside the backpack. "Oh, Ali! Let me see."

Ali rushed over to the table and
unzipped the pocket. Little Genie
climbed out, smoothing her ponytail.

"I forgot," Ali said, biting her lip. "And
the heat helped the color spread! What
am I going to do, Genie?"

"Is it really bad?" asked Genie, sitting down on the edge of the table.

Ali nodded. She pulled out one of the pink and purple jerseys and held it up.

"Wow! That's great!" Little Genie beamed. "What a cool color for a soccer team!"

Ali stared despairingly at her. "But they're supposed to be pale blue and white," she pointed out. "Daniel's going to be really annoyed—and so is the rest of the team."

"I don't see why." Little Genie sounded puzzled. "Pink and purple are way nicer. I bet there aren't any other teams with pink and purple shirts."

"Yes, I bet there aren't," Ali groaned. How was she going to explain this to

Mary? "Come on, Genie, think!" Ali went on urgently. "Mary's going to be back any minute now, and she'll want to know what happened."

Little Genie looked blank for a moment, then brightened. "Well, we could hide the shirts so Mary can't find them," she suggested. "Or I could make them invisible."

Ali bit her lip. Genie wasn't helping at all.

"Hang on a minute," Ali said excitedly as an idea popped into her head. "I've got it!"

"Oooh!" Little Genie jumped up, looking excited too. "What?"

"I'll tell Mary something red must have got into the washing machine, and the color ran and turned everything pink," Ali decided. "That happened to my mom once. She washed one of Jake's dark socks with her white T-shirts and they all came out blue."

"Great idea!" Little Genie exclaimed, dancing about on the edge of the table. "We just need to put something red in the dryer so that Mary believes us."

"Yes, and you're going to have to take care of that," Ali whispered. She was beginning to panic because she could hear Mary's voice out in the hall. "Quick!"

"Leave it to me," Little Genie said confidently. "Hmmm, something red . . . ," she began muttering to herself. Ali hoped she was going to produce a dark red sweatshirt or some really bright socks.

A few seconds later, Genie grinned

broadly at her. "It's done," she whispered with a wink. Then she dived headfirst into the backpack pocket.

Mary came into the laundry room holding a large duffel. "Time to go," she said to Ali. "Is it dry yet?"

Ali felt a blush start at her toes and work its way up to her face. "Um—yes," she stammered. "But there's a bit of a problem."

"What kind of problem?" Mary frowned, raising her eyebrows. She put her hand in the dryer and pulled out a jersey while Ali hovered nearby, shuffling from foot to foot.

"It's pink! With purple stripes!" Mary gasped, holding up the shirt and staring at it as if she couldn't believe her eyes.

"Yes, I know," Ali put in quickly. "I think something red must have got into the washing machine by accident."

Mary started to pull out pair after pair of bright pink shorts. "Daniel's going to kill me," she moaned.

Ali felt bad as she bent down and began to help her friend pull the clothes out of the dryer. She didn't want to get Mary into trouble.

"I think you're right, Ali," Mary went on, pulling out another shirt. "There must be something red in here."

Suddenly two bright red tomatoes dropped out of the shirt in Mary's hand and rolled through the door and across the kitchen floor. Ali and Mary stared at them.

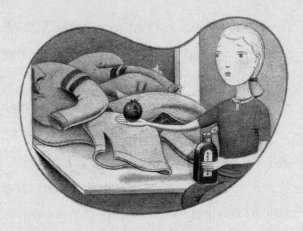

"*T-tomatoes?*" Mary stammered. "What are *they* doing in the dryer?"

Ali tried not to groan. She should never have trusted Genie!

"And look at this!" Mary said in amazement as she pulled out a bottle of ketchup.

Ali couldn't help smiling. Genie had had the right idea. After all, ketchup and tomatoes would certainly make a big red mess. She wasn't sure they'd actually dye anything, though. Luckily, Mary began to laugh.

"This is really weird," she said. "But do you know what, I like these colors together." She held a pink and purple shirt against herself to admire it.

"But what's Daniel going to say?" Ali said anxiously.

Mary grinned, her eyes sparkling. "Who cares?" she replied cheerfully. "I can't wait to see his face when we give him a *pink* jersey to play in." She began to bundle the shirts and shorts into the bag. "It serves him right for making us carry it all to the playing field. Come on. This is going to be fun!"

"Um—yeah," Ali agreed hesitantly,

beginning to fold one of the shirts. But she couldn't help feeling worried. Daniel and his teammates were going to be really mad when they saw their uniforms. And it was all her fault.

Chapter Seven
A Shaggy-Dog Problem

When they'd finished packing the bag, Mary went over to the kitchen door. "Dad, we're ready to go," she called. There was no reply. Mary turned back to Ali. "He must be upstairs," she said. "I'll just go up and get him."

"Is your mom coming?" Ali asked.

Mary shook her head. "She's working late. Will you go and get Nugget for me, please? He loves coming to soccer matches."

"Oh! I can't," Ali began, but it was too late. Mary had already run out of the kitchen and upstairs.

"Who's Nugget?" Little Genie asked, stretching her arms as she poked her head out of the backpack. "Ah, that's better. It's getting a bit boring in here."

"The O'Connors' dog," Ali told her. She went over to the window and peered out into the backyard. Nugget, a big hairy dog with large floppy paws and a long fluffy tail, was snoozing in the shade under a tree. "How am I supposed to get him without turning him pink?"

Little Genie grinned. "I don't know how you could explain *that* away. Still . . ."

She beamed proudly at Ali. "That business with the red things worked just fine, didn't it?"

"Well, sort of," Ali admitted as she remembered the look on Mary's face when the tomatoes had rolled out. "But what am I going to do about Nugget?"

"Oh, you'll think of something," Little Genie said airily. She frowned at the sound of footsteps on the stairs. "Time for me to disappear."

Ali picked up the backpack and zipped Genie into her pocket, then slipped it over her shoulder. Mary and Mr. O'Connor came into the kitchen.

"Let's go, girls," Mr. O'Connor said, picking up the bag. "We don't want to miss the start of the match."

Mary winked at Ali, then frowned. "Where's Nugget? Didn't you bring him in, Ali?"

"I couldn't," Ali explained quickly. "My mom has just found out that she's allergic to dog hair, so . . . so I can't get any on my clothes. It makes her sneeze and her eyes swell." *That sounds believable*, Ali thought.

"Oh." Mary looked surprised. "She always used to play with Nugget. It must have come on very suddenly."

"Well, yes. Yes, it did," Ali agreed. *About two minutes ago, actually!*

Mary picked up Nugget's leash and went outside. She came back a moment later with Nugget trotting happily beside her. As soon as he spotted Ali, he began barking and dragging Mary toward her.

"Hello, Nugget," Ali half shrieked, backing up to keep out of the excited dog's way.

"Stop it, Nugget!" Mary yelled as Nugget jumped up at Ali, trying to lick her nose. Ali held her arms high above her head, hoping Nugget wouldn't manage to lick her fingers. "He can't understand why you're not petting him," Mary puffed, trying to haul the dog away.

Nugget whined and lunged forward again. This time he was too strong for Mary, and the leash slipped through her fingers. Ali gasped as Nugget flew straight toward her, his tail wagging. "Keep away from me!" she cried. In desperation she ran behind an open closet door and dived inside, almost falling over a bucket.

"Stop shaking me, Ali!" Genie yelled from inside the backpack, which had fallen off Ali's shoulders.

"Ali!" Mary gasped. "What are you *doing*? You can come out now. Dad's got Nugget."

Rather sheepishly, Ali crept out of the closet. Mr. O'Connor was chuckling and holding Nugget's leash, and Mary was staring at her in surprise.

"Your mom must be *really* bad if you're that worried about dog hair," she said.

Ali felt very embarrassed. She picked up her backpack.

"Just a minute," said Mr. O'Connor as they went out into the hall. "Can't forget my lucky charm!" He rooted around in the coat closet and pulled out a blue and white striped scarf. "I never go to Daniel's matches without my lucky scarf," he told Ali.

"Those are the team's *usual* colors," Mary pointed out to Ali, her eyes sparkling with mischief. "Pale blue and white. I think they're boring. Maybe it's time for a change, Dad."

"Certainly not," said Mr. O'Connor, sounding horrified. "The Cocoa Superstars have always played in blue and white. Even when I played for them."

"Was that in the old days?" Mary asked. "Before they invented the wheel?"

Mr. O'Connor laughed. "It wasn't that long ago. Now come on or we'll be late."

Ali began to feel even more worried as they all went outside. Mr. O'Connor was right. A soccer team's colors were very important to their fans. What was the crowd going to say when they discovered that their team was playing in pink and purple instead of blue and white? She just hoped the crowd wasn't too big, or there could be lots of unhappy people.

"It's a really big match today," Mr. O'Connor went on as they walked along the street. "The Superstars are playing the Kingston Flyers, our biggest rivals. At least the Superstars will have plenty of people there cheering for them."

Oh, great, Ali thought, her heart sinking.

They turned left and headed down Dudley Street, which was the shortest way to the playing field. Dudley Street was always full of people. Ali had to be very careful to keep her hands in her pockets to make sure she didn't accidentally touch anyone.

She was just congratulating herself on doing rather well when suddenly someone brushed past her, knocking her off balance. It was a young mom pushing a baby in a stroller. A little girl holding a doll was toddling along behind her.

Ali stumbled forward and put her hands out to steady herself. As she did so, her fingers brushed against the doll the little girl was holding. Immediately the doll's skirt changed from yellow to bright pink.

"Oh!" The little girl gasped, staring at her doll with wide eyes. "Mommy, look! Dolly's wearing a pink skirt now. It's magic!"

That's true, Ali thought with a grin. Quickly she ran to catch up with the others, leaving the little girl smiling at her doll's new skirt.

When they reached the playing field, Daniel and the rest of the Cocoa Superstars were waiting impatiently outside the clubhouse.

"This is going to be funny," Mary whispered to Ali.

Ali gulped. *I hope so,* she thought.

"Where've you been?" Daniel asked. "We've been waiting for ages. The other team has already changed."

"Sorry," Mary said. "There was, um, an accident."

"What do you mean?" Daniel looked annoyed.

Mary pointed at the duffel. "You'd better take a look."

Ali held her breath as Daniel unzipped the bag and stuck his hand in. He pulled out a pink and purple shirt, followed by a pair of bright pink shorts.

"They're pink!" he yelled.

Chapter Eight
Superstars and Stripes!

Ali felt very guilty. Daniel and the rest of the team stared in horror.

"What happened, Mary?" Mr. O'Connor asked, his eyes wide.

"Sorry. I washed them with something red," Mary apologized. She caught Ali's eye, and the look on her face made Ali want to burst out laughing.

"Oh, great!" Daniel groaned. The

other guys on the team looked outraged.

"I'm not wearing pink!" one of them said in disgust.

"Hey, what's wrong with pink?" came an indignant voice from inside Ali's backpack. Luckily, no one else heard.

"We'll have to cancel the match," said another member of the team. The others nodded.

"Oh, come on, guys, it's not that bad," said Mr. O'Connor, who looked as if he was trying not to laugh too.

Daniel turned to him. "Dad, a *friend* is coming to watch the match," he protested. "She's going to think I'm totally weird if I walk out in a pink and purple shirt."

"I think they're quite pretty," Mary said.

"Pretty!" Daniel repeated. "Can you

name any soccer team that plays in *pretty pink* shirts?"

Mary smiled innocently. "Well, you'll be the first, won't you?" she pointed out. "You might start a trend."

"And at least the other team will see you coming," Mr. O'Connor added.

The referee, a tall, thin man dressed in a black shirt and shorts, ran over to them. "Come on, boys," he said, blinking a bit in surprise when he noticed the bright pink jersey in Daniel's hand. "We'll be starting in a few minutes, and you're not even changed yet."

"We have a problem with our uniforms," Daniel explained. "Would it be okay if we played in our T-shirts and shorts?"

The referee shook his head. "You know the rules," he called over his shoulder as he jogged back onto the field. "You have to play in full uniform or you forfeit and the other team gets the win."

Daniel turned to the rest of the players. "Well?" he asked, looking at them. "We can't let the Flyers walk off with this match, can we?"

"No," they muttered gloomily, although

some of them sounded as though they wouldn't mind.

"Pink it is, then, boys!" Genie sang from behind Ali's back.

Ali, Mary, and Mr. O'Connor watched as the team shuffled into the changing room.

"I hope it doesn't affect their playing," Ali said anxiously as they joined the crowd of people standing around the field. Lots of them were wearing blue and white scarves like Mr. O'Connor's.

"They'll be fine," Mr. O'Connor said. "Ah, here come the Kingston Flyers."

Wearing red shirts and dark blue shorts, the Flyers ran out to cheers from their supporters. They began to warm up by kicking a couple of balls around.

A few moments later, Mary nudged Ali. "Here come the Superstars," she said.

Daniel and the others were trailing reluctantly out of the changing room. Ali blinked several times and shook her head in despair. The pink uniforms looked even brighter now!

"Come on, Superstars!" roared the fans, shaking their blue and white scarves in the air. But the cheers trailed off into puzzled silence as they noticed what the team was wearing.

Red-faced, Daniel and the rest of the Superstars made their way through the crowd.

"What on earth are they wearing?" one parent mumbled.

"*Pink* shirts?" said another parent.

"What happened to the blue and white ones?" asked a little boy.

When the Superstars reached the field, it only took a second for the other team to comment on their dazzling new colors.

"Hey, look at that!" the Flyers' goalie shouted, roaring with laughter. "The Superstars like pink!"

"Looks beautiful," the Flyers' captain called with a grin.

"Hey, has anyone got any sunglasses?" asked one of the other players. "That pink is giving me a headache!"

Ali couldn't help feeling bad. This was all thanks to her wish. She watched as Daniel and the rest of the Superstars huddled in a circle, their faces grim.

The Flyers were still joking about the Superstars as the teams got into position. But when the match started, Ali was relieved to see that the teasing had just made Daniel's team even more determined to win. They swept down the field from the kickoff and scored in the first minute, leaving their opponents shaking their heads. But the Flyers recovered quickly and raced with the ball down to the opposite end. Only a great save by the Superstars' goalie prevented the Flyers from scoring.

"It's going to be a good game," Mr. O'Connor said. "It's a shame our side is so quiet, though."

Ali glanced around. The Flyers' fans were leaping around and cheering on the opposite side of the field, but the Superstars' supporters were hardly making any noise. Ali could see several people looking sadly at their blue and white scarves and shaking their heads. If they didn't start cheering soon, the Cocoa Superstars might lose. Maybe she could do something to help.

"Um—I need to go to the bathroom," she whispered to Mary. "Is there one in the clubhouse?"

Mary nodded, and Ali hurried off just as a scorching shot from Daniel flew over the Flyers' crossbar, narrowly missing the goal. *Go, Daniel!* she thought. Maybe if the fans gave him some encouragement, he might score a goal.

"Genie?" Ali put the backpack down

on the floor of the clubhouse reception area. It was empty because everyone was outside watching the match. She unzipped the pocket. "Are you okay?"

"No, I'm really bored," Genie grumbled, lifting herself out of the pocket. "It's hot in here, and I can't even see the match."

"I need my third wish," Ali said urgently. "I wish for some pink scarves and stuff for the Superstars supporters."

"Another wish?" Genie brightened up at once. "Sure!" She snapped her fingers, and a bulging gold bag appeared next to the backpack.

Eagerly Ali pulled it open. "This is great, Genie!" she cried. The bag was stuffed with striped scarves and flags in exactly the same shade of pink and purple as the team's uniforms. "Thank you."

"Any time," Little Genie said with a wink. "You'd better take it out there, hadn't you?" She wriggled down into the pocket. "Here we go again," Ali heard her mutter as she did up the zip.

Ali picked up the bag and ran outside. "Look, Mary!" She dashed over to her friend, waving one of the scarves. "I— I found these in the clubhouse."

Mary looked puzzled. "Where did *they* come from?"

Ali shrugged. "I don't know," she fibbed. "But we can give them out to the crowd."

Mary and Ali each draped a scarf around her neck and grabbed a flag. They gave a scarf and flag to Mr. O'Connor, too. Then they ran up and down the bleachers handing out the remaining ones to the Superstars' supporters.

"Thanks," said one man, taking a scarf. He handed a striped flag to his glum-looking son, who cheered up immediately.

"Come on, Superstars!" roared the fans, shaking their scarves and waving their flags.

Just then the whistle blew for halftime. Ali felt very pleased with herself. For once, her wish had put things right. She felt a bit sorry for Genie, though, stuck in the backpack. Maybe if she put it down on the grass and covered it halfway with her jacket, Genie would be able to pop her head out and watch

the second half of the match without
being seen.

Ali put down her backpack and
started to unzip the pocket. "Genie," she
whispered. "You can watch the match
now. Just be careful."

But Genie didn't appear.

Frowning, Ali pulled the pocket open and peered inside. Her heart missed a beat.

The pocket was empty. Little Genie had vanished!

Chapter Nine
Give Me a G!

"Oh no!" Ali gasped. Could Genie have fallen out without Ali noticing? No, the pocket had been zipped shut. So where was she?

Biting her lip, Ali began to search through her backpack. The referee blew his whistle to begin the second half. The crowd let out a cheer as the Superstars almost scored again, but Ali didn't look up. She was too worried about Genie.

"Ali, what are you doing?"

Mary was staring down at her. "Um—I was thirsty," Ali said weakly. "I was just looking for my juice box."

"Well, you're missing the match," Mary said. "And it's really exciting." She broke off to shout, "Come on, Daniel!" as her brother ran down the field, neatly dribbling the ball past two defenders.

Ali frowned. She *had* to find Genie! Maybe she ought to go back to the clubhouse and see if she was there.

Suddenly the sound of laughter and clapping made Ali glance up. Her eyes opened wide. She could hardly believe what she was seeing.

Little Genie was standing on the side of the field, full size. Her hair was in braids. She wore a short swirly pink skirt and a pink T-shirt with matching sneakers, and she held two big fluffy pompoms! As Ali watched openmouthed, Genie began to high-kick her way along the touchline.

"Superstars, Superstars are the best!" Genie chanted. "Superstars, Superstars beat the rest! S-U-P-E-R-S-T-A-R-S!"

The Superstars fans took up the chant. "Superstars, Superstars are the best!" they yelled. And on the field, the pink-clad players surged forward, looking more determined than ever.

Mary nudged Ali and nodded toward Little Genie, who was waving her pom-poms. "Who is that?" she asked.

"Oh, her? I—I think I've seen her around," Ali muttered. She edged away from Mary and Mr. O'Connor and made her way over to Genie. "What are you *doing*?" she whispered.

"Cheerleading, of course!" Genie said, doing a jump. "Here." She paused for a moment and handed a pom-pom to Ali. "Why don't you join in?"

"We'd love to," said a voice behind Ali. Mary was standing there, smiling at Genie. "You look great!"

"Thanks." Genie beamed at Mary and handed her a pom-pom.

Ali gulped. Her best friend and Little Genie—together! For a moment Ali worried that Genie would be banished to her Lava lamp forever—but then she realized she hadn't told anyone about Genie. Genie had just showed up.

Genie, Ali, and Mary stood at the edge of the playing field, and Ali and Mary tried to copy Genie's moves. They side-stepped left and right, then did a series of high kicks, Rockette style.

"Where did you learn all this?" Ali asked Genie as the crowd cheered yet another play by the Superstars.

"Don't you remember that movie we watched last week?" Genie whispered back.

"Oh yes, the one about the cheer-leading squad." Ali laughed. "Come on, Superstars!" she shouted.

Mary gestured across the field with her pom-pom. "Ali, see that girl over there in the red jacket? That's Julie. The girl Daniel likes."

Ali glanced over. The dark-haired girl was staring at the Superstars as if she couldn't believe her eyes.

"I'm not sure she likes the pink uni-forms," Mary said, sounding worried. "I never thought I'd say this, but I hope it doesn't make her not like Daniel. He's phoned her three nights in a row, and that's a record for him."

"Well, in that case, we'd better make sure they win," Genie declared. "That'll impress her. S-U-P-E-R-S-T-A-R-S! Superstars!"

Mary and Ali joined in. There was a deafening cheer as Daniel swept forward with the ball. He dodged one defender, then another, and raced into the penalty area. He took a shot at the goal. The goalie dived the wrong way, and the ball flew into the back of the net.

"Goal!" roared the crowd. Genie, Ali, and Mary jumped up and down, cheering and shouting.

A few minutes later the referee blew

the whistle to end the match. The score was 2–0 Superstars. The fans went wild. As the Flyers trudged gloomily off the field, the Superstars' supporters surged onto it to congratulate the players. In the rush, Ali lost sight of Mary and Genie.

Suddenly Ali felt something tugging on her leg. She glanced down. There was a tiny Genie, dressed in regular Genie clothes, clinging to her jeans. "Help me, Ali!" she called. "Before I get squished!"

Ali bent down and scooped Genie up, shielding her with her other hand as she popped her back into the backpack pocket. Luckily, everybody was too busy celebrating to notice what Ali was doing.

"Look at Daniel and Julie," Genie said with a grin, resting her elbows on the edge of the pocket. The two teenagers were talking. "Do you think it's true love?"

Ali laughed. "Well, I don't think she'll mind about the pink," she said. "Daniel's a hero!"

Little Genie looked thoughtful. "Hmmm . . . maybe I can help him impress her even more! What about a nice bunch of flowers?"

"That's a good idea," Ali began as Genie started another spell.

But then Ali's heart sank. As Daniel spoke to Julie, a thick shower of bright pink flour appeared from nowhere, covering them both from head to toe.

Chapter Ten
Pink Party Time

Julie screamed, Daniel gasped, and everyone else looked around to see two pink, floury figures coughing and wiping their eyes.

"Genie, that's *flour*!" Ali yelped. "Not *flowers*."

"Oops!" Genie said. Her ponytail dipped. "I was never very good at spelling." And she disappeared inside the backpack pocket.

To her relief, Ali saw that Daniel and Julie were laughing as they dusted each other off.

"Did you see that?" Mary grinned, coming over to stand next to Ali. "Where did all that pink flour come from?"

"It must have been a joke by one of the Flyers," Ali suggested.

"Yeah, I suppose so," Mary agreed. "Hey, there's been a lot of pink around today, hasn't there!"

You can say that again, Ali thought.

"Come on, girls." Mary's dad came up to them, his pink scarf still wrapped around his neck. "I've invited the team and their families to come home with us and celebrate. We're going to have a party!"

"Yippee!" Mary exclaimed. Ali let out a sigh of relief. After such a disastrous start, her pink day had turned out pretty well.

The Superstars trooped back to the O'Connors' house to celebrate. Mrs. O'Connor had just arrived back from work. She looked rather surprised to see so many people on her doorstep. But she snapped to attention. "Everyone out on the deck! I'll phone in an order for pizzas."

While Mr. O'Connor was shepherding people out back, Ali and Mary went into the kitchen to help Mrs. O'Connor.

"Hmm, let's see what we can find in the meantime," Mrs. O'Connor said, opening up the cupboards. "It's a bit short notice, but I'm sure we can come up with something."

"Dad went to the supermarket yesterday while you were at work," Mary reminded her mom. "There should be loads of stuff."

While Mary and Mrs. O'Connor were putting out paper plates and cutlery, Ali peeked into one of the open cupboards. There were packages of doughnuts and cookies and bottles of lemonade. Suddenly Ali had an idea. Maybe her pink fingers would come in handy just this once. Quickly she took out the food and bottles. Immediately it all turned bright pink.

"Hey, look over here," she called to Mary and Mrs. O'Connor. "There's lots of food here—and it's all pink!"

"Great!" said Mary eagerly as she helped Ali empty the cupboard. "Hang on a minute. Dad couldn't have known we were going to have a pink party. Wasn't it lucky he bought all this stuff?"

"*Really* lucky," Ali agreed, her eyes twinkling.

Mrs. O'Connor put everything on a tray and carried it out to the crowded deck. A CD was blaring and several people were dancing.

"Hey, Ali," Mr. O'Connor called. "Come and have a dance." He held out his hands, but Ali took a step back in alarm. She didn't want to turn Mary's dad bright pink.

"I—uh—just have to get something from my backpack," she called, racing back inside. When she was safe, she unzipped the pocket and Genie poked her head out.

"It sounds like fun out there," Genie said enviously. "Can I get out and dance?"

"No, you might get stepped on," Ali told her. "Mary's dad wants to dance with me, and I'm scared I might turn him pink!"

"Oh, don't worry about that," said

Genie. "Here, try these for size!" She snapped her fingers, and a pair of thick brown mittens appeared on Ali's hands.

"I can't wear these," Ali gasped. "This is Florida, Genie! And they look like part of a bear suit. What am I going to say when people ask me why I'm wearing them?"

"You'll think of something," Genie said breezily, and disappeared. Then she popped back out. "Oh, can I have one of those pink cookies?"

With a huff, Ali walked back outside, trying to keep her hands out of sight. Luckily, Mary was busy talking to Julie, so she didn't notice the mittens. Ali managed to pick up a pink cookie and stuff it into the backpack pocket, although the huge mittens made it difficult. She hoped Mary's dad had forgotten about dancing with her so that she could take the mittens off, but he was heading toward her again.

"Come on, Ali," he said. Then he stopped and stared. "Where'd you get those? You and Mary playing dress-up?" he asked, raising his eyebrows.

"Not exactly," Ali said, putting her backpack next to a shrub. "My hands were, uh, freezing. I was holding all the cold lemonade and soda bottles."

"Come on, then!" Mr. O'Connor laughed, grabbing Ali's hand and swinging her around. "A dance will warm you up."

Once she was sure she wasn't going to turn Mary's dad pink, Ali began to enjoy herself. They were dancing around to BoyFrenzy's latest song when suddenly a thought struck Ali. She stopped dead and stared down at her hands. *The mittens hadn't turned pink!* They were touching her fingers and yet they were still brown. Did that mean that the wishes were over? Had all the sand run through the hourglass?

"Sorry," Ali said to a startled Mr. O'Connor. "I need to get something from my backpack again."

Leaving Mary's dad dancing on his own, Ali picked up her backpack and headed back inside. She passed Daniel in the hall. He was talking with some of his friends.

"You know, those pink jerseys really brought us luck today," Daniel was saying. "Maybe we should keep them. What do you think, guys?"

His friends nodded and cheered. Quickly Ali ran into the kitchen. There was no one around, so she opened the backpack. A low, rumbling snore floated out. Ali peeked inside and saw Genie curled up, fast asleep and covered in cookie crumbs.

"Genie!" Ali whispered. "I think the wishes have ended. Genie?"

But Genie didn't wake up. She must have been tired out from all that cheer-leading and eating that enormous cookie. Ali grinned. Well, at least everything was back to normal.

But suddenly she noticed the Super-stars' jerseys lying in a heap next to the washing machine. Ali groaned under her breath. Now that her wishes were over, the bright pink color had vanished. They were blue and white again!

"Oh no!" Ali muttered. How on earth was she going to explain *that*? Especially now that Daniel and the team wanted to keep the pink. With a sigh, Ali began shoving the jerseys into Mary's duffel. There was only one thing she could do. She'd have to take them home and *dye* them bright pink.

"Ali?" That was Mary's voice behind her. "What are you doing?"

Quickly Ali pushed the last blue and white shirt into the duffel and stood up. "I thought I'd give you a break from doing laundry," she said feebly. "I thought, well, um, I thought that *I'd* wash the team's uniforms this week."

Mary stared at her. "You don't have to do that!" she exclaimed. "Besides, my part is over. They're supposed to go home with Joey Coles today."

"Oh, but I *want* to." Ali tried to sound as convincing as she could. "It'll make me feel a part of the Cocoa Superstars team. And I'd better get going—I want to make sure they're clean for the next match."

"Well, I think you're bonkers!" Mary laughed. "But okay!"

Ali said goodbye and trudged out the front door, slinging the heavy duffel over her shoulder along with her backpack.

Just as she was thinking that there was no way she could carry the bag all the way home, a flying carpet, with green and pink stripes and golden orange fringe, appeared in front of her.

"Genie!" Ali gasped, putting the backpack down and unzipping it.

Little Genie giggled. "You can't walk home with all this to carry. Better yet, let's fix it right now!" Genie whispered a few words, and when Ali unzipped the duffel, the boys' uniforms were a lovely, dazzling pink. And they smelled great!

"Perfect!" Ali said, running back and dropping the duffel on Mary's front steps. Then she raced back to Genie. "Can we still ride the magic carpet home?"

Genie looked around. The street was empty. "I don't see why not. We'll ride up high, above the trees, so no one will see us."

Ali picked up her backpack with Genie inside and climbed on board. The carpet began to tingle. "There's just one thing," Ali said, pointing to the pink stripe. "Can I wish this was a different color?"

"Nope," Genie said with a smile. "No more wishes until the sand in my hour-glass begins to fall."

Ali held on to the fringe as the carpet began to rise in the early-evening sky. "Well, one thing's for sure. I've had enough pink to last a lifetime!"